THE
KING SHRENIKA OF RAJAGRIHA WAS A PIOUS KING WHO HAD DONE MANY GOOD DEEDS. ONE DAY A DEVA APPEARED BEFORE HIM AND ...
...REWARDED HIM WITH A NECKLACE OF PRECIOUS STONES.
TREAT THIS NECKLACE WITH CARE...
...FOR IF IT BREAKS, THE MAN WHO REPAIRS IT, WILL DIE AT ONCE!

KING SHRENIKA WAS VERY PLEASED TO RECEIVE THE NECKLACE AND HE GAVE IT TO HIS FAVOURITE WIFE, QUEEN CHELLANA.
IT SHINES LIKE THE STARS IN THE MILKY WAY — IT'S HEAVENLY!
IT IS HEAVENLY. I GOT IT AS A GIFT FROM A DEVA.
LOOK AFTER IT WELL.
I WILL. NEVER, EVEN FOR A SINGLE DAY, WILL I PART WITH MY NECKLACE!
QUEEN CHELLANA WORE THE NECKLACE EVERY DAY.
ONE MORNING, THE QUEEN WAS ABOUT TO PUT ON THE NECKLACE...

... WHEN THE STRING GAVE WAY.
OH, MY BEAUTIFUL NECKLACE!
THE QUEEN'S MAID CAREFULLY PICKED UP THE PRECIOUS STONES STREWN ON THE FLOOR.
THE KING WILL BE ANGRY WHEN HE HEARS OF THIS!
DON'T WORRY, MY QUEEN. HE WILL SOON HAVE IT REPAIRED.
BUT WHEN THE KING WAS INFORMED, HE WAS VERY DISTURBED.
I DON'T THINK WE CAN HAVE YOUR NECKLACE REPAIRED.
BUT WHY NOT?
BECAUSE THE DEVA, WHOSE GIFT IT WAS, WARNED ME THAT THE MAN WHO REPAIRS THE NECKLACE WILL DIE THE MOMENT THE WORK IS DONE.
I MUST HAVE MY NECKLACE. I CAN'T DO WITHOUT IT!

IT IS OUT OF THE QUESTION. I CAN'T RISK THE LIFE OF ANY OF MY SUBJECTS!
YOU ARE SAYING THIS ONLY TO AVOID PAYING A REWARD FOR THE REPAIR OF THE NECKLACE!
THE KING TURNED HELPLESSLY TO HIS MINISTER, ABHAY KUMAR.
WOMEN ARE SO UNREASONABLE! HOW CAN I LIE ABOUT THE FATE AWAITING THE MAN WHO REPAIRS THIS NECKLACE? WHO WOULD THEN BE SO FOOLHARDY AS TO ACCEPT SUCH AN OFFER?
THE FATE THAT AWAITS WHOEVER REPAIRS THE NECKLACE MUST NOT BE HIDDEN, MY KING.
EXACTLY! SO WHAT'S THE USE OF OFFERING A REWARD?
ISSUE A PROCLAMATION ANY WAY, AND THEN LET'S SEE WHAT HAPPENS.

THE NEXT DAY THE KING'S CRIERS ANNOUNCED THE REWARD —
ONE LAKH OF GOLD COINS FOR STRINGING QUEEN CHELLANA'S NECKLACE!
ONE LAKH! JUST FOR STRINGING A NECKLACE?
I'LL DO IT!
AND I!
BUT, REMEMBER, THE MAN WHO COMPLETES THIS TASK WILL DIE IMMEDIATELY AFTER.
OH! THEN IT'S NOT FOR ME!
NOR ME!
FOR A LONG TIME NO ONE CAME FORWARD TO DO THE WORK. THEN AN OLD GOLDSMITH WHO WAS VERY POOR, DECIDED TO ACCEPT THE KING'S OFFER.
I AM AT THE END OF MY LIFE IN ANY CASE. IF I DIE TO EARN THE REWARD, MY DEAR SONS WILL BENEFIT!
SO THE GOLDSMITH ASKED FOR PERMISSION TO SPEAK TO THE KING.
FRIEND, I AM HAPPY YOU HAVE AGREED TO DO THIS SERVICE FOR THE QUEEN.

THE KING TURNED TO HIS GUARD —
GIVE HIM THE CASKET CONTAINING THE PRECIOUS NECKLACE.
HERE IS A PART OF THE REWARD. THE REST WILL BE PAID WHEN THE WORK IS COMPLETED. I HOPE YOU SUCCEED.
WITH GOD'S HELP, MY KING, I HOPE TO SUCCEED.
THE GOLDSMITH RETURNED HOME WITH THE CASKET AND TOLD HIS SONS WHAT HE HAD DECIDED TO DO.
FATHER, DON'T DO IT!
YOUR LIFE IS WORTH A LOT MORE TO US THAN THE MONEY.
DON'T TRY TO STOP ME, MY SONS. MY MIND IS MADE UP.

ONLY REMEMBER, WHEN I HAVE COMPLETED MY TASK AND I AM NO MORE, TAKE THE NECKLACE TO THE KING AND CLAIM THE REST OF THE REWARD.
THE GOLDSMITH THEN SHUT THE DOOR AND BEGAN HIS WORK. SPREADING THE SPARKLING JEWELS IN FRONT OF HIM, HE PREPARED TO THREAD THEM. BUT —
OH! OH! THIS IS AN UNEXPECTED PROBLEM.
IT'S IMPOSSIBLE TO STRING THESE STONES. THE HOLES ARE SO TINY, ONLY AN ANT COULD GO THROUGH THEM!
...AN ANT! THAT'S IT! I HAVE AN IDEA!
FIRST, I'LL DIP ONE END OF THE STRING IN HONEY...

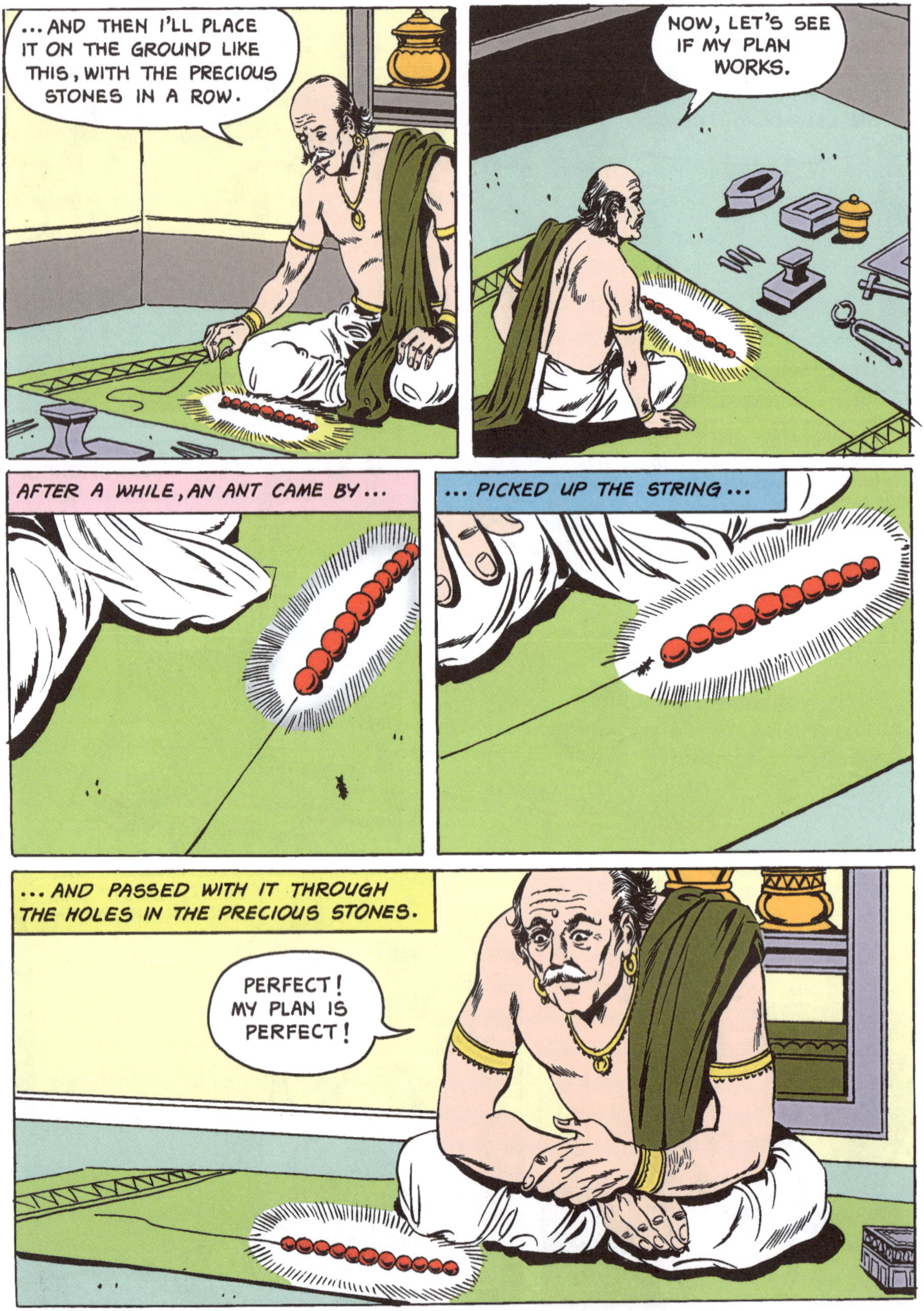
...AND THEN I'LL PLACE IT ON THE GROUND LIKE THIS, WITH THE PRECIOUS STONES IN A ROW.
NOW, LET'S SEE IF MY PLAN WORKS.
AFTER A WHILE, AN ANT CAME BY...
...PICKED UP THE STRING...
...AND PASSED WITH IT THROUGH THE HOLES IN THE PRECIOUS STONES.
PERFECT! MY PLAN IS PERFECT!

WHEN THE ANT FINALLY EMERGED WITH THE STRING FROM THE LAST STONE...
...THE GOLDSMITH PICKED UP THE TWO ENDS AND FITTED UP THE CLASP.
HE HELD UP HIS BEAUTIFUL HANDIWORK AND REJOICED IN IT FOR JUST ONE MOMENT.
THE NEXT MOMENT, HE WAS DEAD.
THE FOUR SONS OF THE GOLDSMITH MOURNED THE DEATH OF THEIR FATHER.
POOR FATHER!
HE LOVED US MORE DEARLY THAN LIFE ITSELF!

AFTER SOME TIME, REMEMBERING THEIR FATHER'S LAST WORDS, THE FOUR BOYS TOOK THE CELESTIAL NECKLACE TO KING SHRENIKA.
THE NECKLACE HAS BEEN REPAIRED! GOOD! THE QUEEN WILL BE DELIGHTED!
THEN MAY WE HAVE THE REST OF THE REWARD?
REWARD? BUT WHERE IS THE OLD MAN WHO REPAIRED THE NECKLACE?
THE OLD GOLDSMITH WAS MY FATHER. AS SOON AS HE HAD REPAIRED THE NECK-LACE, HE DIED, AS WAS FATED.
HE TOLD US TO COLLECT THE MONEY FROM YOU AFTER HIS DEATH.

BUT HOW DO I KNOW YOU ARE REALLY HIS SONS? FOR ALL I KNOW YOU MAY HAVE STOLEN THE NECKLACE FROM THE POOR OLD MAN!
BUT, SIR... !
GO AWAY, BEFORE I HAVE YOU PUT INTO MY DUNGEONS!
SADLY, THE GOLDSMITH'S SONS LEFT THE KING'S PALACE.
ONE IS POWERLESS AGAINST A KING ....

SOME YEARS LATER, THEY WERE PASSING THROUGH A FOREST.
POOR FATHER! IF HE KNEW THE KING REFUSED TO PAY US THE MONEY HE WOULD BE VERY UNHAPPY.
NOW, THE OLD GOLDSMITH HAD BEEN REBORN AS A MONKEY. THIS MONKEY CHANCED TO BE SITTING ON A TREE ABOVE AND, HEARING THEM, THE MEMORY OF HIS PAST LIFE FLASHED UPON HIM WITH BLINDING SUDDENNESS.
AH, MY DEAR SONS! SO THE KING HAS DONE YOU OUT OF THE REWARD I PAID FOR SO DEARLY!
THE KING HAS NO RIGHT TO THE NECKLACE. TILL HE PAYS FOR THE WORK, IT BELONGS TO MY SONS.
I MUST GET HOLD OF THE NECKLACE.

THE MONKEY WENT TO THE PALACE, WONDERING HOW HE COULD GET HOLD OF THE NECKLACE.
IF I GO INTO THE PALACE, I WILL BE SPOTTED AT ONCE. I WILL WAIT OUTSIDE NEAR THIS TANK.
NOT LONG AFTER THIS, QUEEN CHELLANA CAME TO THE TANK TO BATHE.
SHE PLACED HER NECKLACE AND OTHER ORNAMENTS IN THE CARE OF HER MAID.
WAIT HERE TILL I RETURN FROM MY DIP IN THE TANK, KAPILA. WE WON'T BE LONG.
THE MONKEY WAITED TILL THE QUEEN HAD LEFT AND THE MAID, KAPILA, WAS ALONE.

THEN HE SWOOPED DOWN SO SWIFTLY ...
... AND PICKED UP THE NECKLACE SO DEFTLY ...
... THAT THE MAID NOTICED NOTHING.
THE MONKEY THEN WENT TO HIS OLD HOME ...

...AND THREW IN THE NECKLACE.
CLUNK!
WHAT'S THAT ?
IT'S THE CELESTIAL NECKLACE!
ONE OF THE GOLDSMITH'S SONS SPRANG TO THE WINDOW AND SAW THE MONKEY.
THERE'S A MONKEY HERE! HE MUST HAVE BROUGHT THE NECKLACE!
DON'T BE ALARMED, SON. IT IS I, YOUR FATHER. I WAS BORN AGAIN IN THIS FORM....

HIDE THE NECKLACE. THE KING HAS NO RIGHT TO IT TILL HE PAYS THE PROMISED REWARD.
THE SONS WERE AFRAID TO KEEP THE NECKLACE, BUT —
THERE'S NO NEED TO BE AFRAID. DO AS I SAY AND ALL WILL BE WELL.
FAREWELL, MY SONS.
THE BOYS DECIDED TO BURY THE NECKLACE IN THE HOUSE.
THIS PLACE SHOULD BE QUITE SAFE.
WE'LL DIG A HOLE HERE.

THERE! WE'VE FINISHED! LET'S PUT THE CHARPOY OVER IT.
NOW THE PATCH OF DUG EARTH IS WELL HIDDEN.
MEANWHILE IN THE PALACE GARDENS —
KAPILA, WHERE'S MY NECKLACE?
NECKLACE...? IT... IT'S GONE...!
YOU ARE TREMBLING, KAPILA! WHY SUCH FEAR? I KNOW YOU COULDN'T HAVE TAKEN IT!
NO, INDEED, I HAVEN'T.

BUT THE NECKLACE WAS TAKEN AND YOU NOTICED NOTHING ? STRANGE ! WERE YOU HERE ALL THE TIME ?
I'VE BEEN SITTING RIGHT HERE SINCE YOU LEFT !

I CAN'T UNDERSTAND IT. BUT THE KING WILL FIND THE ANSWER. LET'S GO BACK TO THE PALACE.

THE CELESTIAL NECKLACE HAS BEEN STOLEN ? WE'LL FIND IT SOON ENOUGH. SUCH A UNIQUE NECKLACE CANNOT BE HIDDEN FOR LONG.

HE TURNED TO HIS VIRTUOUS MINISTER.
DON'T YOU AGREE, ABHAY KUMAR?
YES. IT SHOULD TAKE LESS THAN A WEEK TO FIND THE THIEF.
THEN GET TO WORK AS SOON AS POSSIBLE. FIND THE THIEF AND RECOVER THE NECKLACE.
I WILL ORDER AN IMMEDIATE SEARCH IN THE CITY.
SOME TIME LATER—
NO SIGN OF THE NECKLACE YET?
NO. WE'VE RANSACKED THE HOUSES OF ALL THE KNOWN THIEVES...
...AND WE ARE CERTAIN THEY ARE INNOCENT OF THIS CRIME.
WHAT'S MORE, THEY WERE SHOCKED THAT ANY ONE DARED TO TAKE THE CELESTIAL NECKLACE. THEY KNOW IT IS IMPOSSIBLE TO SELL SUCH A NECKLACE.

HMM ... THE NECKLACE HASN'T BEEN STOLEN BY A REGULAR THIEF, THAT'S CERTAIN. WHOEVER TOOK IT HAD ANOTHER MOTIVE FOR DOING SO.
ABHAY KUMAR REPORTED TO THE KING.
THE NECKLACE WILL BE DIFFICULT TO RE-COVER. WHOEVER TOOK IT, HAS NO INTENTION OF SELLING IT.
AS THERE SEEMED TO BE NO OTHER WAY OF RECOVERING THE NECKLACE, THE KING ISSUED A PROCLAMATION.
THERE IS A DEATH SENTENCE AWAITING THE MAN WHO TOOK THE QUEEN'S NECKLACE ...
... BUT IF HE COMES FORWARD AND SURRENDERS THE NECKLACE, HE WILL BE GRANTED A FULL PARDON.
OH ! MY SONS SHALL NOT GIVE UP THEIR CLAIM SO EASILY.

THE MONKEY WENT TO SPEAK TO HIS SONS, AND FOUND THEM BUSY DIGGING UP THE HOLE AGAIN. THEY HAD ALREADY HEARD OF THE KING'S PROCLAMATION.
WE HAD BETTER RETURN THE NECKLACE BEFORE WE ARE DISCOVERED!
LET'S DO IT SOON. I AM AFRAID....
NO, DEAR SONS. DON'T RETURN IT. GIVE ME THE NECKLACE. I'LL TAKE CARE OF THIS MATTER.
THE MONKEY CARRIED AWAY THE NECKLACE TO THE FOREST.
ALL DAY LONG HE HID IN THE HOLLOW OF A TREE.

AT SUNSET HE VENTURED OUT AGAIN AND CAME TO A PARK NEAR A TEMPLE.
I MUST THINK OF A SAFE PLACE TO HIDE THIS NECKLACE.
JUST THEN, ACHARYA SUHASTI, A RENOWED ASCETIC, EMERGED FROM THE TEMPLE...

...AND, STANDING UNDER THE SAME TREE, WAS LOST IN MEDITATION.
FOR A LONG TIME THE MONKEY WATCHED THE ASCETIC. THEN A THOUGHT SLOWLY DAWNED ON HIM —
THE ASCETIC IS AN HONEST MAN. WHERE ELSE COULD THE NECKLACE BE MORE SAFE THAN ON HIS NECK?
SO HE PLACED THE NECKLACE ROUND THE NECK OF THE ASCETIC...
...AND WENT AWAY, WELL SATISFIED.

THAT NIGHT, THE KING'S MINISTER, ABHAY KUMAR, WAS PRACTISING AUSTERITIES IN THE TEMPLE IN THE COMPANY OF ACHARYA SUHASTI'S DISCIPLES.
AT THE END OF THE FIRST QUARTER OF THE NIGHT, SHIVA, THE DISCIPLE WHO HAD BEEN ATTENDING UPON SUHASTI, RETURNED TO THE TEMPLE.
FEAR EXISTS
WHY IS HE SAYING THAT INSTEAD OF THE USUAL SALUTATION, "ALL IS WELL"? I MUST ASK HIM TO EXPLAIN.
SURELY AN ASCETIC HAS NOTHING TO FEAR?
TRUE, BUT I WAS ONCE A HOUSEHOLDER AND I HAVE EXPERIENCED FEAR. I RECALLED THE FEELING AGAIN JUST NOW.
BUT WILL YOU TELL ME ABOUT THE FEAR YOU EXPERIENCED IN YOUR LIFE AS A HOUSEHOLDER?
SHIVA NARRATED HIS LIFE'S STORY.

AS SHIVA WAS FINISHING HIS STORY, THE SECOND QUARTER ENDED AND THE DISCIPLE, SUVRATA, WHO HAD BEEN ATTENDING UPON SUHASTI, ENTERED.
GREAT FEAR
ON ABHAY KUMAR'S ENQUIRY, SUVRATA TOO RECALLED AN EPISODE IN HIS LIFE WHEN HE HAD EXPERIENCED FEAR.
AT THE END OF THE THIRD QUARTER OF THE NIGHT, THE DISCIPLE, JAYANA, WHO HAD JUST COMPLETED HIS TURN OF ATTENDING ON THE ASCETIC, RETURNED.
EXTREME FEAR
ABHAY KUMAR ASKED HIM, TOO, TO TELL HIS STORY.
JUST AS JAYANA HAD FINISHED HIS STORY, THE FOURTH QUARTER OF THE NIGHT ENDED, AND THE DISCIPLE, DHANNYA, RETURNING FROM HIS DUTIES WITH SUHASTI, UTTERED THE STRANGE WORDS —
FEAR, EXTREME FEAR
AND DHANNYA, LIKE SHIVA, SUVRATA AND JAYANA, TOLD ABHAY KUMAR AN EPISODE IN HIS PAST WHEN HE HAD EXPERIENCED EXTREME FEAR.

IT WAS MORNING WHEN THE LAST DISCIPLE FINISHED HIS TALE. THE DEVOUT PRIME MINISTER PREPARED TO DEPART.
AS HE MADE HIS WAY OUT —
THE QUEEN'S NECKLACE!
AH, NOW I UNDER-STAND WHY THEY SENSED FEAR! FOR AN ASCETIC, THE SIGHT OF WEALTH IS FEARFUL BECAUSE IT IS THE CAUSE OF ALL THE WORLD'S EVILS.
BUT THE SAGE IS NOT AFFECTED BY THE NECKLACE. HE IS CALM. HE HAS ACHIEVED COMPLETE DETACH-MENT.
I DON'T KNOW HOW THE NECKLACE CAME TO BE ROUND THE GOOD ACHARYA'S NECK, BUT I KNOW THAT HE COULD NOT HAVE STOLEN IT.

HE UNHOOKED THE CLASP...
... AND TOOK THE NECKLACE BACK TO THE KING.
YOU HAVE FOUND THE NECKLACE! WHERE IS THE BOLD THIEF WHO TOOK IT?
THERE WAS NO THIEF, KING. I FOUND IT ROUND THE NECK OF ACHARYA SUHASTI.
SUHASTI, OUR PURE SAGE! YOU MUST BE JOKING.
THE NECKLACE WAS SPARKLING ROUND THE SAGE'S NECK, WHILE HE WAS COMPLETELY UNAWARE OF IT AND DEEP IN MEDITATION.

THERE IS SOME MYSTERY BEHIND THIS ....
YES. SOMEONE, IT APPEARS, WANTS TO DRAW YOUR ATTENTION TO AN IN-JUSTICE CONNECTED WITH THE NECKLACE.
THE OLD MAN WHO REPAIRED THE NECKLACE DID NOT TURN UP FOR THE REST OF THE REWARD — DO YOU THINK THAT HAS ANYTHING TO DO WITH THE THEFT OF THE NECKLACE?
THE OLD GOLD-SMITH MUST HAVE DIED THE MOMENT THE NECKLACE WAS REPAIRED.
THAT'S TRUE. YES, NOW I REMEMBER! THAT'S THE REASON HE WAS NOT GIVEN THE REST OF THE REWARD!

BUT HIS SONS CAME AND YOU DENIED THEM THE BENEFIT OF THEIR FATHER'S WORK.
KING SHRENIKA WAS LOST IN THOUGHT FOR A WHILE, THEN —
QUEEN CHELLANA WAS NOT SO WRONG, AFTER ALL. THOUGH I DID NOT ADMIT IT EVEN TO MYSELF, I DID NOT WANT TO PAY A REWARD.
A KING MUST BE A FATHER TO HIS SUBJECTS WHEN THEY ARE IN HARDSHIP, YET I WITHHELD FROM THOSE POOR BOYS WHAT WAS THEIR DUE!
SEND FOR THE GOLDSMITH'S SONS AT ONCE SO THAT I CAN MAKE AMENDS.

THE GOLDSMITH'S SONS WERE OVERJOYED WHEN THEY RECEIVED THE MESSAGE THAT THE KING HAD REALISED HIS MISTAKE.
THE KING IS A GOOD MAN.
NOT FOR NOTHING DID THE DEVA GIFT HIM WITH THE CELESTIAL NECKLACE.
SOONER OR LATER HE WAS BOUND TO COME TO HIS SENSES.

ON THEIR WAY TO THE PALACE, THEY HAD TO PASS THROUGH THE FOREST. THE MONKEY SAW HIS SONS.
MY DEAR SONS! THEY ARE LOOKING HAPPY. I WONDER WHERE THEY ARE GOING?

THE MONKEY FOLLOWED THEM AT A DISTANCE INTO THE PALACE GARDEN.
I AM SORRY I DOUBTED YOUR WORD. YOUR FATHER WAS A WORTHY MAN AND A GOOD CRAFTSMAN.

HERE IS THE REWARD. TAKE IT AND LIVE A LIFE WORTHY OF YOUR GOOD FATHER.
THANK YOU, KING SHRENIKA. YOU ARE INDEED JUST.
MY MISSION IS SUCCESSFUL! MY SONS ARE WELL CARED FOR NOW.
HOW HAPPY I AM TO HAVE MY BEAUTIFUL NECKLACE BACK!

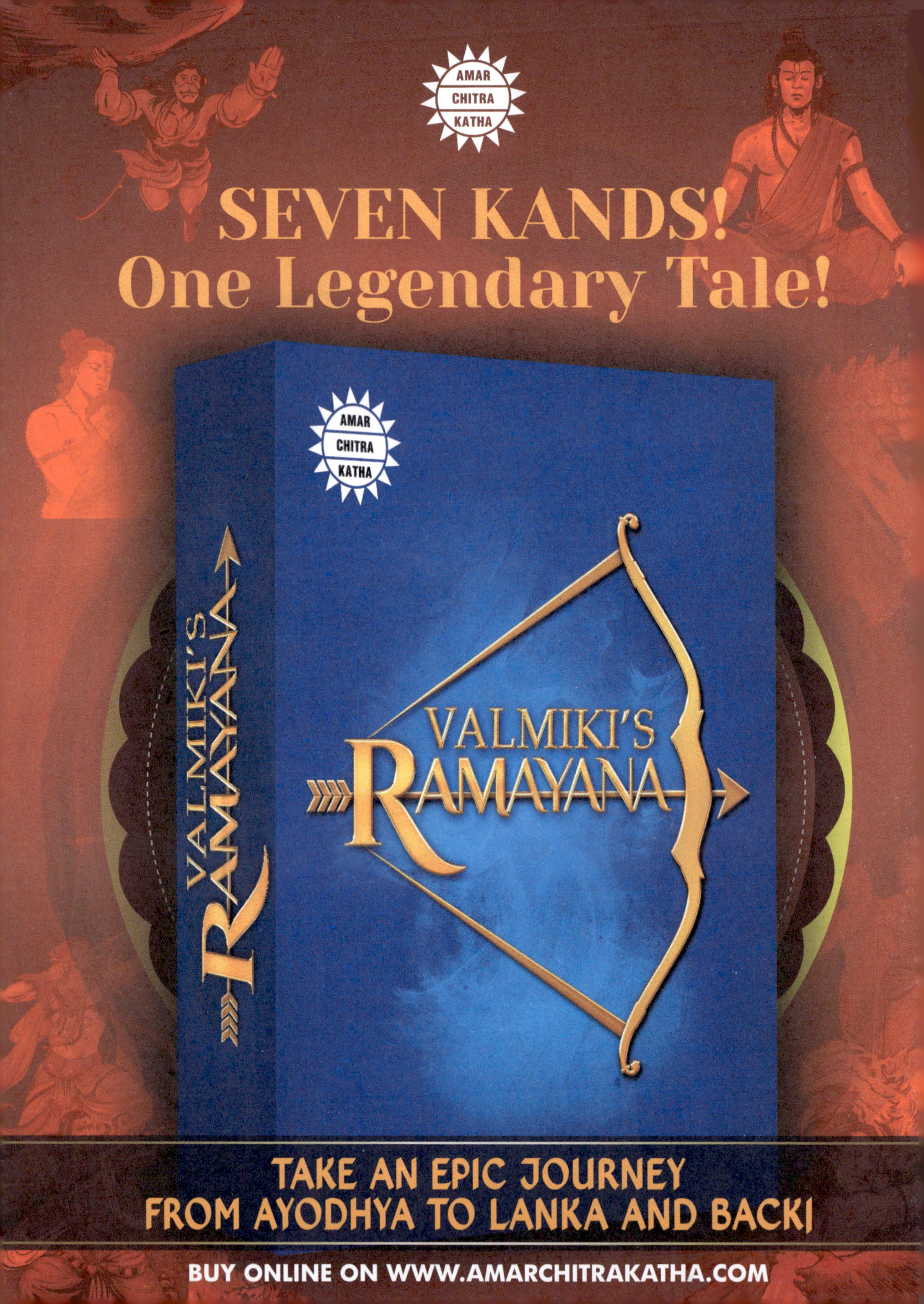
AMAR CHITRA KATHA
SEVEN KANDS!
One Legendary Tale!
AMAR CHITRA KATHA
VALMIKI'S RAMAYANA
VALMIKI'S RAMAYANA
TAKE AN EPIC JOURNEY
FROM AYODHYA TO LANKA AND BACK!
BUY ONLINE ON WWW.AMARCHITRAKATHA.COM